MW00916347

Written by Linda Copeland
Illustrated by Lindy Burnett

In a field where flowers bloom on a beautiful sunny day,
Meet our friend Bitsy with her Happy Bouquet.

Her bouquets are presents for family and friends;
Look, see the many reasons for the bouquets she sends.

And, find Caterpillar Sam who is looking with you;
He's spying on Bitsy and finding the reasons, too.

With her girl friend Corey,
Bitsy plays and has fun.
Bitsy's bouquet shows Corey
she's her friend number one.

Classmate Tommy Foster,
is sick and home in bed;
Bitsy sent him flowers--
to cheer him, she said.

Her grandmother is most special,
Bitsy loves her so much;
Her happy flower bouquet
is her sweet loving touch.

Bitsy's big brother Bobby
went to a formal affair;
He sent his date a corsage
to wear in her hair.

The happy bride at Bitsy's church
is coming down the aisle;
The bride's bouquet of Bitsy's
flowers makes everyone smile.

abc

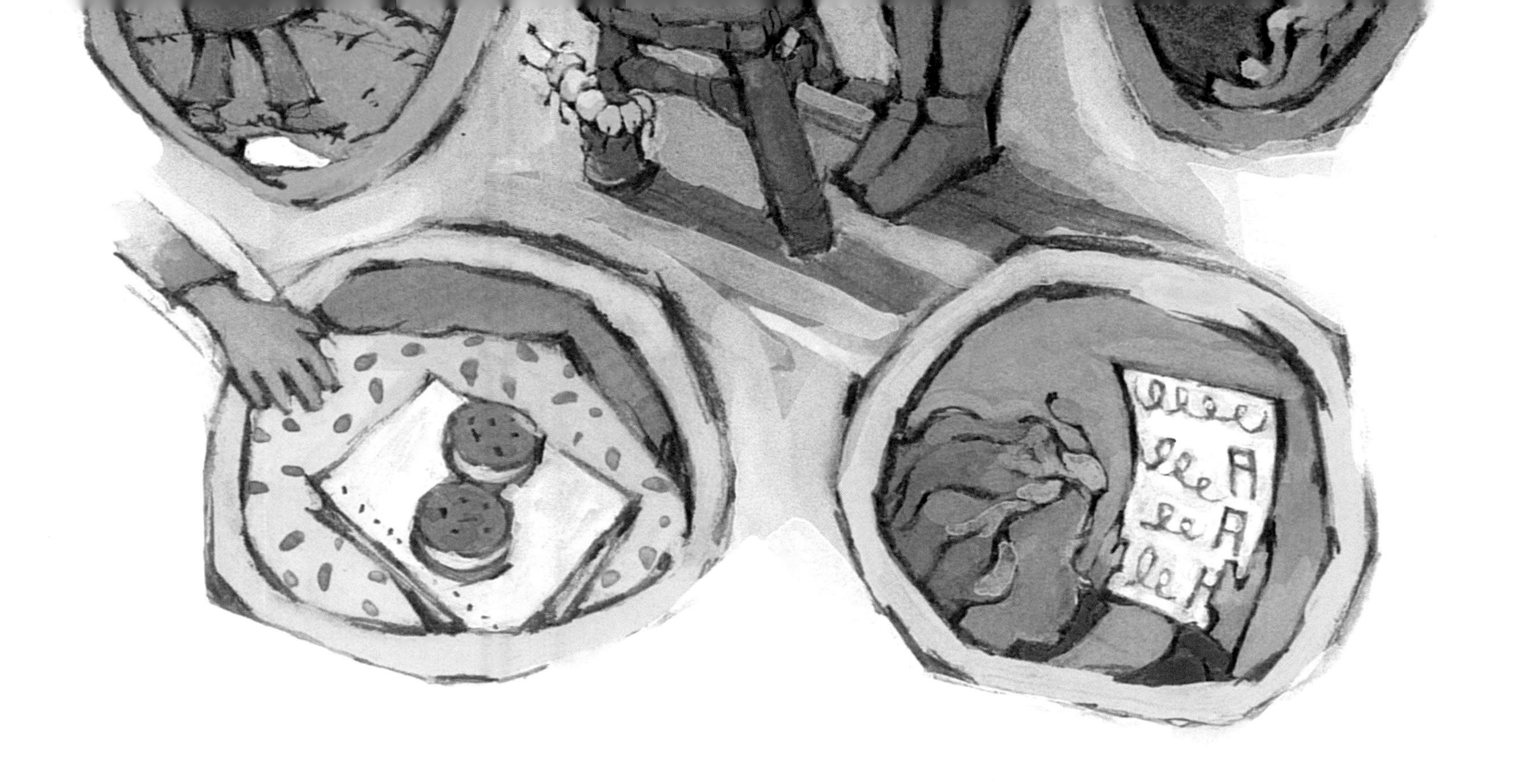

To her teacher, Miss Lucy,
Bitsy gives a daisy chain bouquet,
A circle of flowers to say thank you
for her happy school day.

Flowers add cheer to holidays: family times and celebrations.
Bitsy's bouquet for Thanksgiving is the centerpiece decoration.

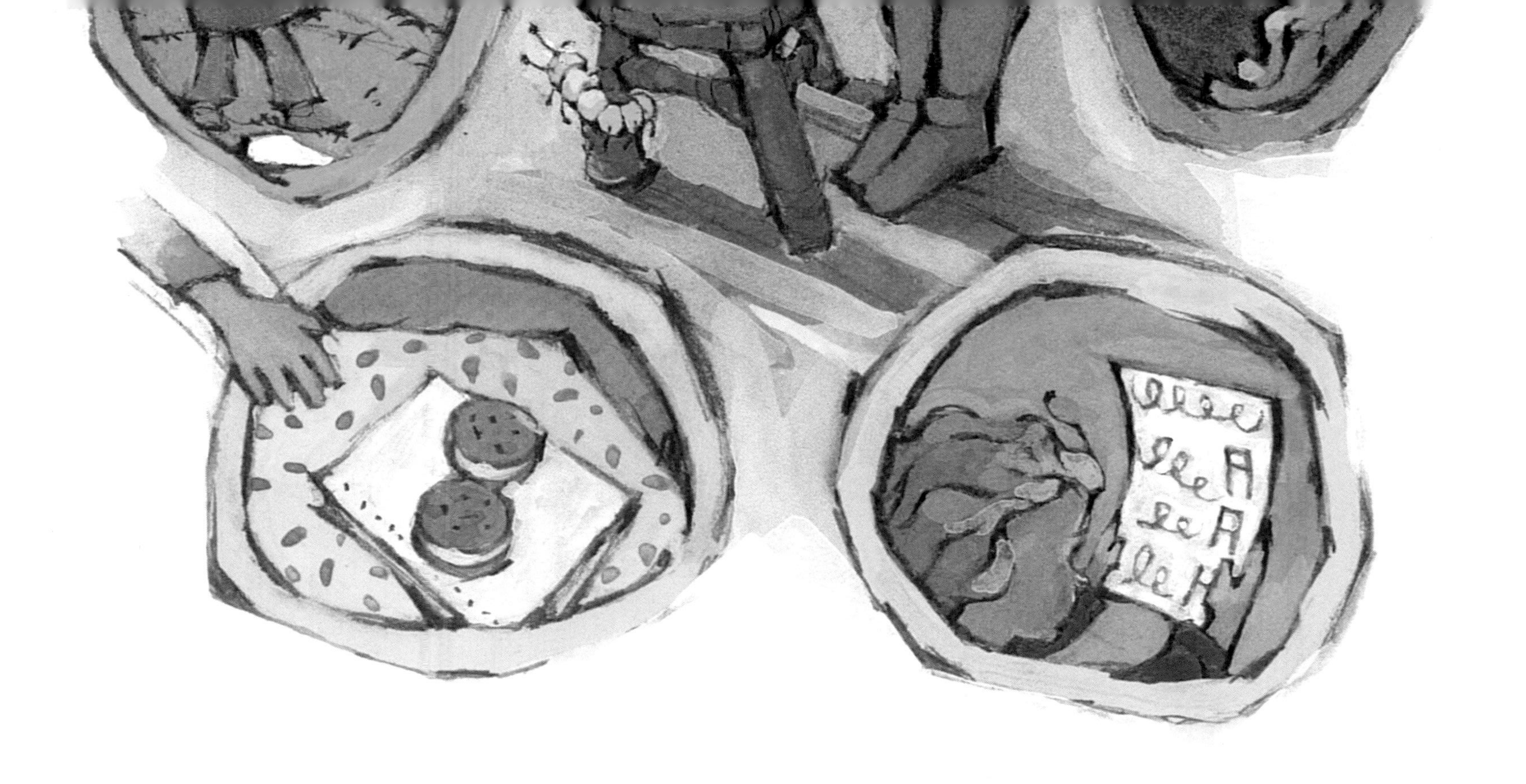

To her teacher, Miss Lucy,
Bitsy gives a daisy chain bouquet,
A circle of flowers to say thank you
for her happy school day.

Flowers add cheer to holidays: family times and celebrations.
Bitsy's bouquet for Thanksgiving is the centerpiece decoration.

Bitsy's parents are honored on their special days each year.
Bitsy gives each parent flowers – with her love so dear.

At parties with her friends
she enjoys dancing and singing;
Bitsy's thank you to the hostess
is the bouquet she is bringing.

HAPPY

Bitsy's sister Susie loves to dance ballet;
At Susie's recital, Bitsy gave her a beautiful bouquet.

Big sister, Kim,
graduates today;
Bitsy's note and flowers
are on the way.

Bitsy's next door neighbor
has a sweet little girl;
Bitsy took her flowers
as a welcome to the world.

FLOWERSHOP
Closed

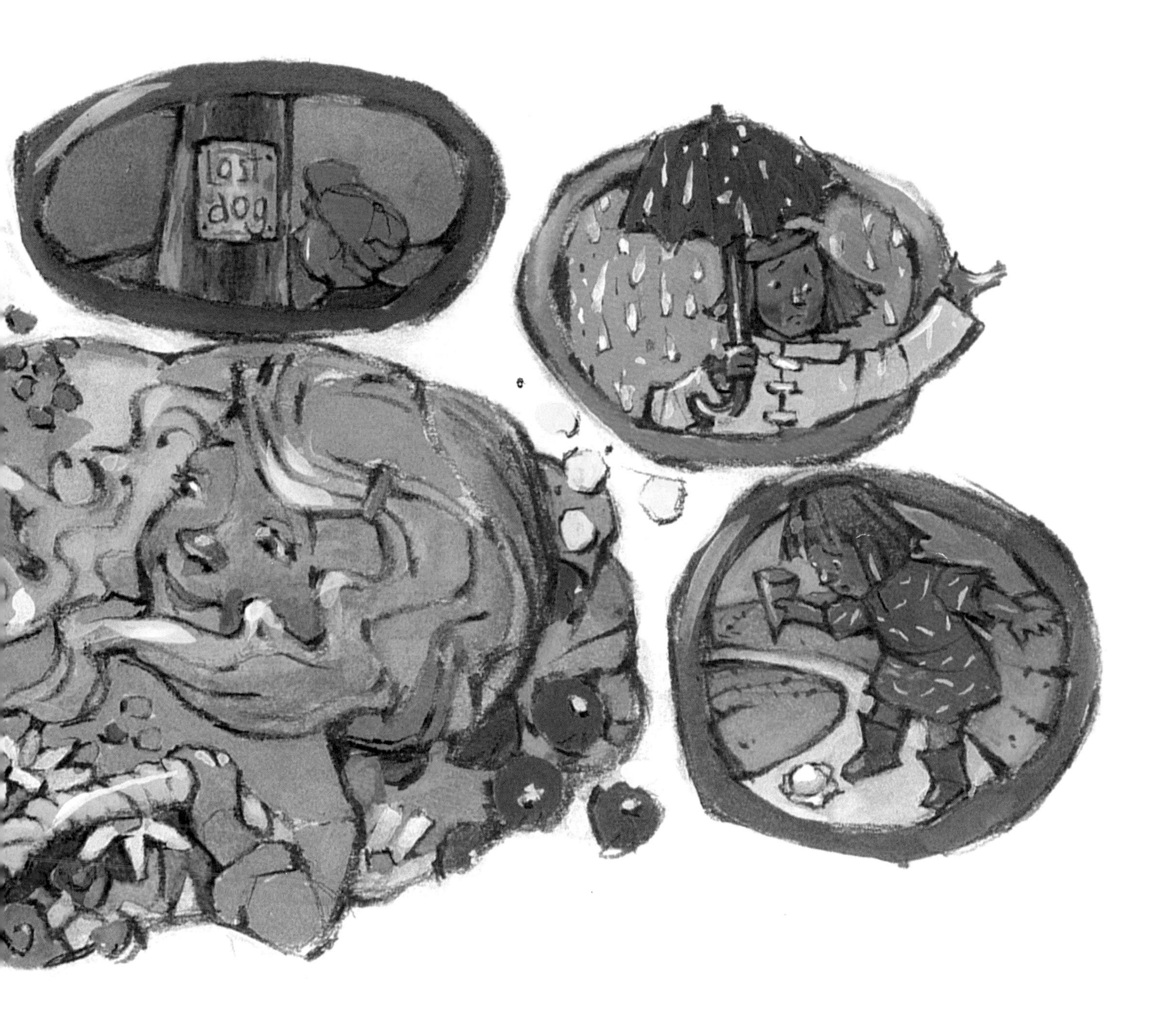

When people are sad and need others' love and care
Bitsy's thoughtful bouquets have a warm message to share.

Bitsy's parents' anniversary
dinner is happening tonight;
Her flowers for the table
are sure to delight.

Sometimes careless words and
deeds cause others pain;
Bitsy's potted flowers say,
"Sorry; it will not happen again."

Bitsy's birthday has come, and,
oh my, for goodness sake
Her mother put her bouquet
in the middle of her cake!

Friendship
Birthday
Apology
Anniversary
Sickness
Love
Dating
Wedding
Thank You

Bitsy has found many reasons
to give her Happy Bouquet.
How many did you count
for what the flowers say?

Caterpillar Sam says,
"Show others you care in this beautiful way."

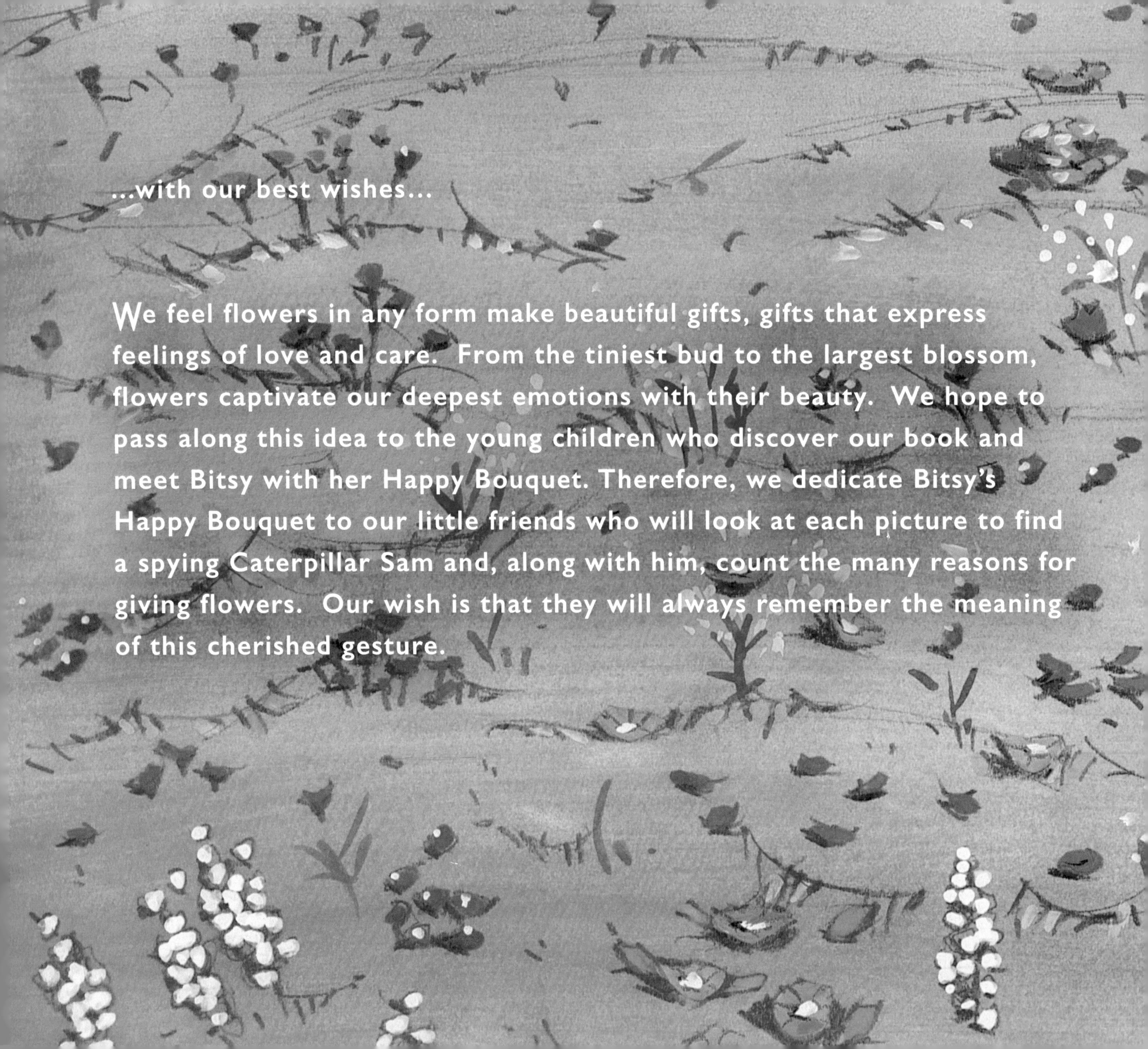

...with our best wishes...

We feel flowers in any form make beautiful gifts, gifts that express feelings of love and care. From the tiniest bud to the largest blossom, flowers captivate our deepest emotions with their beauty. We hope to pass along this idea to the young children who discover our book and meet Bitsy with her Happy Bouquet. Therefore, we dedicate Bitsy's Happy Bouquet to our little friends who will look at each picture to find a spying Caterpillar Sam and, along with him, count the many reasons for giving flowers. Our wish is that they will always remember the meaning of this cherished gesture.

Always loving flowers and gardening, Linda Langston Copeland desires to share her passions with children everywhere. After graduating from Wheaton College in Norton, Massachusetts, and after her children were grown, Linda returned to school to study horticuture at the University of Georgia. She is co-author of *Legends in the Garden* and for over two decades has coordinated worldwide garden tours for Garden Vistas. Living in Atlanta, GA, Linda has been an active volunteer for many gardening-related organizations. She and her husband, Dean, have a son and daughter and three grandsons.

Lindy Burnett has illustrated award winning ad campaigns for numerous Fortune 500 companies but her greatest passion is creating art with children in mind. She has illustrated several children's books of note, and has found tremendous inspiration in the mind's eye of kids. Lindy and husband Rob spend time between the glorious little town of Madison, Georgia and Cocoa Beach, Florida. They have five remarkable grown kids and five grandkids as well!

Bitsy's Happy Bouquet

Library of Congress Cataloging-in-Publication Data

Printed in the United States of America, 2015

Copeland, Linda
Bitsy's Happy Bouquet/Linda Copeland;
Illustrations by Lindy Burnett; graphic design by Janie Hester

ISBN 978-1-4951-8749-0
10 9 8 7 6 5 4 3 2 1

1. Children's literature 2. Flowers